Evguénie Sokolov
A Parabolic Tale

by

SERGE GAINSBOURG

Translation by
John and Doreen Weightman

TamTam Books
1998

First published in France in 1980
by Editions Gallimard.

English translation ©Virgin Books 1980.
Introduction© bart plantenga 1998.
Afterword © Russell Mael 1998.
©1998 TamTam Books.

TamTam Books are edited and published by
Tosh Berman.

TamTam Books
2601 Waverly Drive
Los Angeles, CA 90039-2724

tosh@loop.com

First Editon
ISBN 0-9662346-1-8

Library of Congress Catalog Card Number: 97-
80957

Serge Gainsbourg: The Obscurity of Fame

"Man created god. The inverse remains to be proven."

In January of 1969 (after DeSade but before Prince) a song exploded in the face of an unsuspecting pop universe-- "Je T'Aime...Moi Non Plus." The singer-provocateur: Serge Gainsbourg. Partner in crime: English actress (Blow Up) and heartthrob, Jane Birkin. The effect: mayhem and scandal. The magnitude: somewhere between Elvis' censored pelvis and the tragedy at Altamont. Journalists, world politicians, even the Pope condemned the song as immoral. There were calls for stricter

censorship, the review of pop lyrics.
The single was banned in Sweden,
Spain, Brazil, and Britain. The Vatican
implores the Italian government to ban-
ish it. Phillips is forced to stop pressing
the disc. The slack is however, instantly
taken up by various black market firms.
It appears in 8 languages including
Japanese. And with every shrill denun-
ciation comes increased sales, exceeding
2 million by winter's end. Gainsbourg is
one of Europe's biggest pop acts.

    But Gainsbourg, with typical
blasé bohemian elan, just grins, insists it
is just an enjoyable sex spoof. And all
this downside sure looks like up to him.
In familiar mythic terms he's 1 part rat
pack, 1 part beatnik, Chet Baker,
Sinatra, a dash of Dylan, Leonard
Cohen's pungent growl, Tom Waits'
irrepressible inventiveness, Johnny

Rotten's naughtiness, the look of an absinthe abuser. Actor, pianist, singer, raconteur, poet, filmmaker, soundtrack composer, photographer, painter, novelist but always the rascal voice of the desire dispossessed.

"Je T'aime" has been covered by many, including Donna Summer and Barry Adamson (Nick Cave and the Bad Seeds). In 1975 he directed his first film, "Je T'Aime...Moi Non Plus" with Warhol star of Trash, Joe Dellesandro, Jane Birkin and a young, unknown Gerard Depardieu.

Gainsbourg mastered the art of scandal better than anyone, including Malcolm Mclaren, because it was written into his DNA -- Born To Raise Hell; he just couldn't help it. "For me provocation is oxygen." He once said. He enjoyed his notoriety but still managed

to seduce people with his humanity.
With his cig-dangling-from-lips, lecher-
ous persona, his poignant lyrics, and
nihilism he was able to speak the
unspeakable, once even proclaiming, "I
wanna fuck you," to Whitney Houston
on live TV. He walked that jittery
tightrope between outcast and pop star
-- marginal yet marketable; every indie
rocker's dream -- or scheme.

      Gainsbourg was the kind of cul-
ture hero that seldom exists in America.
His death of a heart attack on March 2,
1991, for instance, warranted something
of a national day of mourning in France.
But Gainsbourg remains almost totally
invisible in America, a misunderstood
rumor at best despite the recent efforts
by Luna, Luscious Jackson, and Mick
Harvey (also of Bad Seeds fame) whose
English versions of Gainsbourg songs

on his Intoxicated Man reminds us how little we know about him.

"The idea to make this record began from a combination of personal curiosity about Gainsbourg's material (particularly his lyrics) and a growing bewilderment that his work is virtually unknown outside French speaking countries." Mick Harvey explains in his liner notes.

Gainsbourg was born Lucien Ginzburg in 1928 to Russian immigrants in Paris. His father Frenchified their Jewish name and Lucien became Serge Gainsbourg. His father played piano in Pigalle night clubs and Gainsbourg grew up with him playing Bach, Chopin, Stravinsky, and Gershwin at home. Gainsbourg took up piano at a young age. And his father, bubbling with enthusiasm, insisted that young Serge accompany him at the piano in Deauville's casinos and grand hotels. He was all of 8 and painfully shy. Excited by his son's interest in the arts, he enrolled Serge in art school near Montmartre, where Gainsbourg found himself roaming the exotic and tacky streets; dreaming and peeking into the clubs and bordellos. During World War II his family, as Jews, were forced to wear the yellow star. In 1941, his father arranged for falsified papers which allowed them to escape to Limoges. Gainsbourg was marked not only by the yellow star and the horrors of Nazism, but by the ease with which neighbors became cowards -- and collaborators. This would affect him for the rest of his life.

After the war, Gainsbourg, now 19, continued his ramblings through

seedy Pigalle. He grew increasingly dis-
illusioned, gloomy, aimless -- a true cafe
existentialist. He landed numerous
deadened jobs in the area, including
hand-coloring cinema publicity photos,
played classical music at snooty balls
but also played jazz in various smoky
Pigalle dives.

A turning point came in the late
50s when his father landed him a gig in
the hottest club in Paris, the Milord
Arsouille where his idol, Charles Trenet,
got his start. Gainsbourg devoured
Django Reinhardt, Thelonious Monk,
Art Tatum; sees Billy Holiday, Dizzy
Gillespie and even Screamin' Jay
Hawkins live. Years later he pays tribute to Hawkins with his "Mambo Miam
Miam." Gainsbourg however, doesn't
get his first break until 1958 when, upon
hearing him perform live, Boris Vian

(jazz critic, trumpeter, poet, novelist, and social agitator) writes a glowing review of a Gainsbourg gig.   Suddenly Gainsbourg is faced with the notion that he has great potential.

This propelled him headlong into songwriting which he had always despised. But now he can't seem to stop; his songs dealt with his dissipated sur- roundings: alcohol, love, poets (Rimbaud, Prévert, Baudelaire), bohemia, love lost, everyday life. Vian's praise won him his first contract. He produced the 45 "Le Poinçonneur des Lilas," a Goya-like portrait of a train conductor punching tickets all day long. Early song titles reveal his other con- cerns: "Alcohol," "12 Gals Under My Skin," "This Mortal Boredom" -- all "Jazzistiques," or heavy-into-jazz tunes of pop existentialism. Like Bob Dylan's

early ability to fuse blues, French poet-
ry, and the scene's Zeitgeist Gainsbourg
absorbed the day's chaotic cultural,
musical, and political currents to create
art in the form of a unique "voice."
Gainsbourg even reinvented Dylan's
"Ballad of Hollis Brown." Also like
Dylan, Gainsbourg's early fame was
due to poppier interpreters of his songs,
himself claiming, "I thought I was too
ugly to sing them myself." It began with
Les Freres Jacques covering "Lilas" in a
manner not unlike how Peter, Paul and
Mary covered "Blowin' In The Wind."
Other pop stars took notice and record-
ed his songs: Juliette Greco, Petula
Clark, Claude François, France Gall,
Michele Arnaud, Catherine Sauvage,
Françoise Hardy, Dutronc, Brigitte
Bardot, Dalida, Deneuve and even
Isabelle Adjani among many others.

Jacques Brel suggested he start singing
more himself. He did. By 1960
Gainsbourg was heavily into rock and
roll. "Requiem Pour un Twisteur" is his
tribute to its silly liberational possibili-
ties. In 1963 he "introduces" the electric
guitar sound to France. The intrepid
Gainsbourg, with his voracious appetite
for sound, introduced French audiences
to "new" musics -- soul, reggae, hippy
guitar solos -- during his entire career.
He infused his tunes with rock and roll,
mambo, Afro-Cuban rhythms ("Couleur
Cafe"), the Symbolist and rebellious
poets he admired and interpreted: de
Musset, Nerval ("Le Rock de Nerval"),
Baudelaire (Le Serpent Qui Danse"). His
ears devoured Stan Getz and Astrud
Gilberto. By which he drenched his
chansons in heavy saxophone and sul-
try Brazilian samba and pursued the

dramatic tension of feverish emotion that sizzles just beneath cool vocals. In 1964 Gainsbourg, in his own words "impregnated by American music," achieved his biggest vocal development -- the introduction of Anglo-slang (most deliriously evident in "Ford Mustang"). This enlarges his palette, gives him new ammo, new freedom to scat and pun, poke fun, undermine expectation. All these influences, in his throat, become his own.

He emerged more and more the outrageous scoundrel, a devil-may-care idiot-savant who inspired with his ability to foment hilarious controversies, getting away with pranks we only dream of, even as he croaked his way out of the role of singer-songwriter and into that of cultural icon. "Without controversy it would all be very boring."

He observed. In 1967 he began dueting
with chanteuse-actresses not particularly known for their singing abilities, con-
verting their liabilities into charming
attributes. Anna Karina (famous from
early Godard films) helps him
discover the sing-and-respond tension
of the eternal man-woman conflict.

Then a bombshell -- he, the eternal
disheveled scruff, begins work with the
very image of voluptuousness -- Brigitte
Bardot.

This only magnifies his mythic
stature. Their first hit, the enduring and
hilariously breathtaking "Bonnie and
Clyde" continues to seep into our psy-
ches via the recent sampling of MC
Solaar and Renegade Sound Wave. In
the highly inventive (pre-virtual reality)
"Comic Strip" Gainsbourg invites
Bardot into his comic while she ululates

all the POWs and Sh-bangs one sees in comic strip balloons. Their "Harley Davidson," a true outlaw ode to insouciant posturing -- "Hey, what the hell you doin' on my Harley?" Gainsbourg grunts at Bardot straddling a Harley in leather hot pants, assuring us all that the coming revolution will be a sexy one.

In 1968 he met the love of his life, Jane Birkin, on a film set. And there you have it -- crusty old perverted rebel meets innocent gal. She takes France by storm with her heroically flawed pronunciations of French. This offers Gainsbourg another witty tool for wringing meaning from language. He added female choruses, ala Otis Redding, to inject sarcastic responses to his bravado. He eventually dispensed with singing altogether, to develop his latter day signature tobacco-alcohol-inflected gravelly talk over, sometimes employing sarcastically heavy, heaving Kostelanetz-style string sections, at other times foregoing musical accompaniment altogether.

He got the lead in Cannabis, did the soundtrack and dedicated it to Jimi Hendrix and Bela Bartok. He's named "Don Juan of the Year" by various women's magazines. Then wrote several songs influenced by Nabokov, seemingly mirroring his real-life affair with Birkin -- "Jane B" is best described as Lolita + Chopin.

In 1975 his album "Rock Around the Bunker" ruffled feathers because he hurled his legendary sarcasm at political ghosts. Gainsbourg insists that Nazism does not stop at the German border, and pokes fun at I-love-a-man-in-uniform chic. He, a Jew who wore the yellow star, is denounced as anti-semitic. Gainsbourg is by now everywhere -- TV, film, scandal sheets, he publishes a novel, has a photo exhibit, does more soundtracks -- at least everywhere in France.

In 1976 he became the first white guy to do major recording in Kingston, Jamaica, beginning a long stint with the great reggae rhythm duo, Sly Dunbar and Robbie Shakespeare. He also employs Marley's Wailers. In 1979, a feisty Gainsbourg produces "Aux Armes Etcetera," which parodies the militaristic overtones of the "sacred" "La Marseillaise," to a reggae beat, much the way Hendrix reconfigured the "Star Spangled Banner" as antiwar song. Denunciations by generals, priests, and politicians follow. Former paratroopers

and crusty war vets protest at his con-
certs, threaten fans. In Marseilles the
protests led to cancellations. In
Strasbourg, a bomb threat and 400 paratroopers vowing vengeance spooked
the Wailers so much that they refuse to
play. So Gainsbourg took the stage
alone, singing "La Marseillaise"
without musical accompaniment. The
goons join in to sing along and after-
ward file meekly from the hall.

Gainsbourg has charmingly
blind sided them. His album sells over
500,000 copies, goes gold -- his first. He
wins"best male performer" and "best
album" awards at that year's music
awards in Cannes. "Evguénie Sokolov,"
his first novel, describes the turbulence
of this time. "Evguénie Sokolov" is also
a great nose-tweaking "song" -- a series
of farting sounds, "scat flatulence" if

you will, set to a reggae beat.

In 1984 "Love on the Beat" touches on homosexuality and incest. "Beat" is a homonym for "bite" which is French slang for penis. This is not lost on his audience.

In 1985 he does the notorious video "Lemon Incest" with young daughter, Charlotte -- in a bed. The delirious provocations continue. But by now he's more than a singer, he's a national treasure that refuses to stop tarnishing. His scatological and buffoonish sense of satire still offers youth a prime tool for resisting the stultifying aspects of a normal consumer existence. Even the dilapidation of his physical body through self-abuse became a kind of heroic dissipation, a sabot tossed into the gears of the proverbial assembly line. "I have succeeded at everything except my life." He once wistfully said. At the time of his death, March 2, 1991, I thought of how self-depricatingly and appropriately wrong he was.

(first appeared in CUPS Dec. 1996)

bart plantenga

The mask falls, the man remains and the hero fades away.

Serge Gainsbourg

On this hospital bed, over which dung flies are hovering, images of my life come back to me, sometimes clear, sometimes blurred, out of focus as photographers say, some overexposed and others on the contrary quite dark, and if they were placed end to end they would make up a film at once grotesque and horrific, since it would have the peculiarity that the soundtrack, parallel to the longitudinal perforations along its edge, would emit nothing but explosions of intestinal gas.

The sad truth is, if I can trust my uncertain memory, that from a very early age I must have possessed the inborn gift, nay the iniquitous affliction, of constantly breaking wind. But, being by nature both bashful and crafty, I no doubt waited to utter my parasitic

Evguénie Sokolov

sighs at a suitable moment, privately
and without shame, and so none of the
people around me ever suspected my
distressing complaint. I suppose that,
by stealthily relaxing my anal sphincter,
I released hydrogen, carbon dioxide,
nitrogen and methane into the empty
air of water closets and public squares,
and certainly at that time I could with-
hold the noxious fumes at will by a simple contraction of the rectal cavity.

Now, confined to bed and anx-
iously awaiting a third attempt at electrocoagulation, I can see the sheets bil-
lowing up with my tempestuous and
noisome gases, over which, alas, I have
long since lost control and, while spraying the air with ineffectual deodorants, I
retrace the course of my wretched an
nauseous destiny. My first, anally emitted, infant gurglings did not in the least

alarm my wet-nurse, a milk dispenser with deluxe breasts, into whose face I would systematically return, on the draught of my anal wind, the talcous nebulosities she dabbed on my buttocks, since, while I farted, I continued to suck, squeezing a plastic toy rat with a bewildered grin.

Then came a succession of nannies, like an elaborate mannequin parade. One, incidentally, taught me the Cyrillic alphabet, another moss stitch and stocking stitch, and yet a third to play the harmonium, but none of them lasted for more than three months in the face of the powerful odors released by my own wind instrument.

At school, in the seatless latrines with swinging doors (only the master had a key, as if his deposits were more precious), both my throat and my anus would contract with fear at the thought of allowing my parasitical noises to escape and cause a din audible in the playground, although it must be said that the other occupants to judge by their abrasive use of newspaper, had no such inhibitions about disclosing their secret business.

Ignoring the boys playing with knuckle-bones, marbles and tops, pursuits which require the sitting position so conducive to the breaking of wind, and avoiding games of hide and seek in which farts unfailingly betrayed my presence, as well as hopscotch because my knicker-bockers billowed out at every jump, I would disappear on the Trans-Siberian Express as the masterful driver of its imaginary engine and, with the chugging gait of a congenital idiot, I

Serge Gainsbourg

would take it across swaying viaducts and through endless tunnels, punctuating the run with luscious puff-puffings and fart-fartings, forms of escapism so delicious that they sometimes lined my underpants with mustard poultices.

I showed an early and unmistakable aptitude for drawing, although the spontaneity of my sketches and the naive freshness of my watercolors were immediately quelled by the teachers, who had no patience with my cubic balloons, checked rabbits, blue pigs and other embryonic phantasms, and, since I had to bow to authority, I would get my own back at the swimming bath by going close to them and releasing iridescent bubbles, which rose gurgling to the surface and burst into the clean air as subversive farts.

In the dormitory, the problem

was how to break wind freely without
waking anyone up. However, on the
first night, after firing two or three vol-
leys that I managed to disguise by sim-
ulated coughing fits, I instinctively hit
on the solution, which was to insert one
finger gently into my sphincter so that
the wind escaped without causing any
disturbance, and during the day, while
absent-mindedly construing Catullus,
Quid dicam gelli quare rosea ista labella, I
would let off as many sotto voce farts as
I liked, while staring pointedly at the
boys next to me, and such was my self-
possession that no one suspected the
smell to have emanated from me, and
when I was summoned to the black-
board the teacher would sometimes
punish the whole class with detention,
after failing to discover which of his
young rascals was letting off stink-

bombs.

During the holidays, I would escape on my own to Nordic sand dunes and there, shivering in the twilight gusts, I would play the meteorologist, sending up weather balloons which emerged from my fundament, and the wind would carry off my exhalations and disperse the diabolical will o' the wisps in fascinating, enchanted swirls.

I was expelled from school for unruliness, and my winds drove me in the direction of the Ecole des Beaux Arts where, although weak in advanced mathematics, I opted halfheartedly for architectural studies. Now I had to pull myself together, because the classes were mixed. I thus learned to control myself to some extent, without being in any way cured; since the studio was on the sixth floor of an annex of the Beaux

Arts, I made a point of breaking wind at every step, and so managed to contain myself for a period which saw me move on, wind and all, from trigonometry to painting.

I began with charcoal-drawing, and at the crack of dawn would set up my easel near Cellini's *Perseus*, since I was fascinated by the severed throat of the Medusa and, in the often deserted echoing back to me between the bronzes and the plaster casts, reverberated loudly under the glass roof, I felt to some degree happy. Soon I had to move on to live models, and it was with a cold eye, unmoved as yet by any animal complicity, that I discovered the female nude. The mounds of flabby flesh, the swollen or bony bodies, the pubic areas, dun-colored, russet or raven-black, sometimes with the string of a tampax

Serge Gainsbourg

sticking out at the acute angle of the
isosceles triangle, combined to make me
wildly and indelibly misogynistic, at
the same time as my hand idealized it
all in sharp and furious sketches which,
once back home, I initialed with fine
sprinklings of sperm, exhausting auto-
graphs which led me instinctively to a
little suburban prostitute - Rose, Ruby
or Angelica, a name like that of a
flower, a precious stone or a plant, no
matter - who took my penis into her
mouth, where upon I let off a snorter of
a fart which caught the poor wretch
with her head under the sheet, like
someone inhaling under a towel to clear
the nasal passages, and promptly anaes-
thetized her, so that she slid slowly
down onto the linoleum.

Quite soon, I acquired great technical mastery, which however was not

equaled by my ability to control my wind, but I was so keen on my work that I would clench my teeth, nip my buttocks together and feel shivers running up and down the back of my neck, before finally rushing out of the studio into the icy corridors, there to release whole sequences of inopportune and thunderous farts.

I regarded my masters with secret contempt, in spite of the renown they had won through their personal achievements; I appreciated neither the neoclassicism of some nor the retrograde modernism of others, nor the obligation to address them as Maître or Master, which made me feel like a seventh-century Negro slave, and it was only much later that I came to be grateful to them for having initiated me into so noble an art.

At that time, in order to educate my artistic taste, I opted to study in museums. Keeping well away from the *Mona Lisa*, whose ghastly leer warned me that, through some kind of witchcraft, she had had wind, so to speak, of my disability, I would meditate on Mantegna's *Sebastian*, waiting in front of the picture until the museum attendants had moved away before starting up my moped and then, while expelling my exhaust fumes far from the din of traffic, I would admire the firmness of the drawing, the rhythmic pattern of pillars and arrows and the extreme softness of the coloring, which helped to give a trance-like quality to the martyr's death-throes.

Until then, I had succeeded, without too much embarrassment, in keeping myself at a misanthropic distance from my fellowmen, but now, unfortunately, the time came for me to do military service. My medical inspection was a noisy affair, during which the army doctors took my disability as a sign of insubordination, and dispatched me at once to a disciplinary camp. There, in the communal life of the army hut, I came to realize the unfathomable coarseness of men who, as soon as they find themselves shut up together in idleness, make it a point of honor to emit the most repulsive smells through all their natural orifices, not excepting their pores. My soldierly gases filled my companions with hysterical delight and, encouraged by the poor diet - bully-beef, corned-beef and beans - the poor devils developed quite a competitive spirit. "There we go!" some would exclaim as they discharged their ballast.

"Number 2's not far off!", and soon the air would be unbreathable.

Having been declared all-round champion, I was nicknamed the Scent-Bottle, Whizz-Bang, the Gunner, the Artificer, the Artillery-man, Ding-Dong, the Trench-Mortar, the Gas-Bomb, the Bazooka, Big Bertha, Rocket, High Wind, the Blower, the Anesthetist, the Blow-Pipe, the Leak, All-Spice, the Goat, the Skunk, Pit-Gas, Gasogene, Wind in the Willows, Arsenic and Old Lace, Borgia, Zephyr, Sweet Violet, Windy-Windy, Mister Pong, Fart Minor, Stinker, Pipe-Line, Gas Container, Gun-Cotton, Arse Wind, Gas-Oil and the Big One, not to mention other terms I have now forgotten. On the verge of suffocation, and with the sole aim of getting a room to myself, I asked to see the Colonel who, overcoming his aversion to my Slav origins, granted me the privilege, to which my secondary education entitled me, of joining a course for reserve officers, from which I graduated as a sub-lieutenant, only to lose this rank a week later - "Not officer material", as the Sokolov report specified, "Imitates the gun salute during the raising of the flag" - because I had fired a salvo while on parade, a misdemeanor that might have passed unnoticed if the bugler, having breathed in my laughing gas just before putting his instrument to his lips, had not produced, with brassy amplification, sounds more or less identical with those I usually emitted through the anus, thus finding himself sentenced to two weeks' close arrest, a punishment that I myself had to inflict upon him.

I was released from my military

duties one pearly November morning during maneuvers, and I went sadly down the hill, leaving behind me men lying in wait for a hypothetical enemy, flesh and lead soldiers whose taunts I had endured for so long, and in that place, mingling with the bursts of automatic rifle fire and the smack of mortar shells slicing off the tree-tops in the little wood nearby, my farewell farts, my civilian gases, became more acid and embittered than ever.

I went back to my studio, with its musty smell of linseed oil and turpentine, and at once settled down to work. To begin with, my drawings were reminiscent of Goya and Ingres, then, being subject to depression and self-doubt and unable to break away from the influence of Klee, I found refuge in purely technical problems and under took to improve and sharpen my visual acuity by working on living models. But after twelve months of military service, during which I had never tried to control my wind - indeed, the contrary had been the case - it turned out that I was no longer in command of myself and that my gases might issue embarrassingly forth at any time, and so, in order to pursue my work in a relaxed state, I acquired a bull-terrier with pink-rimmed eyes (crimson-lake would, perhaps be more accurate), whom I called Mazeppa and proposed to use as an alibi. I pretended to scold him every time I broke wind, and would call out in a peremptory voice, audible above the uproar, "Mazeppa, how dare you?", and the dog became a most precious asset, first in my relationships with my mistresses, who were torn between the attractiveness of a young artist whose importance they could vaguely sense, and their active disgust with an animal whose appearance repelled them and whose performances they abominated; then in public places, such as restaurants, pubs, buffets and bars, where I would shower insults on the dog. Having very quickly learnt that, after fifteen or twenty farts and the same number of bawlings out, he was entitled to expect a titbit, he maintained a stolidly British demeanor, merely allowing his ear and tail to droop, as if to add greater veracity to my perfidious and cowardly accusations.

At the age of twenty-three, after squandering the meager inheritance left me by my late father on vintage cars and nocturnal escapades, I was faced with the necessity of earning some money. Thus it came about that my pathological disorder gave me the idea of creating a comic strip character who, after being turned down several times by various publishers, became a best seller under the name of Crepitus Ventris, the Jet-Man, copyright Opera Mundi, a new Batman propelled by his own wind, which I indicated by stars of pain, oblong bubbles or explosive balloons emerging from his heroic posterior, and in which I inscribed according to my moods the words: Zoop! Vroosh! Wham! Pow! Swish! Vraoum! Vavoom! Plomp! Whew! Foom! or Flutter! But, so as not to harm my career as a painter, I adopted the nom de plume of Woodes Rogers, who was in fact a real English buccaneer who, in 1712, wrote an account of a journey round the world; on reading it a few year's previously, I had been struck by a sentence to the effect that he had discovered a black pepper called malaguetta, which was very effective in curing wind and preventing colic. And so, being now free from financial worry, I once more settled down to my painting. I soon acquired such technical proficiency that I felt able, as Delacroix had advocated, to sketch a workman falling from a roof in the time it takes him to fall; but one day, while I was testing my mastery by practicing the drawing of sewing needles with a single movement of the pen- a down stroke, then an upward stroke to open the eye, followed by a down stroke to close it - a particularly violent explosion of wind broke a pane in the glass roof, causing my hand to shake like that of an electrolytic child. After contemplating the pieces of broken glass scattered at my feet, I looked up at my drawing and was suddenly transfixed. My arm had functioned like a seismograph.

On analysis, the dazzling beauty of the line seemed to be the product of a sensibility dangerously heightened by some chemical stimulant such as ephedrine, orthedrine, maxiton or corydrane, since it bore a striking resemblance to the electro-encephalographs of epilectics, with an exact correspondence between their paroxystic waves and the peaks of its pattern.

I immediately repeated the experiment by placing my pen, charged with India ink, upright on the paper and waiting for the next fart. It proved to be so overpowering that it drew a jagged line, twenty-five centimeters long, across the sheet of Canson and even tore the paper towards the end of the stroke.

I compared this pattern with the previous one and had to acknowledge the exhilarating truth: my method showed itself to be devastatingly effective. Not only did it retain the individuality of my style, but also, by adding an aggressive heightening, it suggested the possibility of an infinite number of combinations. Nor was there any hint of schizophrenic frenzy expressing itself in a chaotic and fragmentary manner through uncoordinated sensations and feelings because, during the outburst, I had not felt my hand to be completely out of control, so firmly rooted were both my aesthetic sense and my mastery as a draughtsman.

So, as I said to myself during the dark hours of the night while trying in vain to get to sleep, the pestilential exhalations prophetic of my corporeal death were to serve the purpose of channeling and transcending that which was more pure, most enduring and most despairingly ironical in the inner depths of my creative mind, and after all the years devoted to the technique of painting and all the days spent releasing my gases in front of museum walls radiant with the genius of the great masters, these jagged, fragile and tortuous lines had now rid me forever of my inhibitions.

The next morning I gave up using the traditional stool and, with the help of screws and a spanner, fitted to the top of a metal tripod a bicycle seat with coil springs, the mechanical reactions of which gave my perch a variable power of amplification and the sensitivity of a finely tuned seismograph. Thirty days later I was in possession of forty gasograms, fifteen of which I had touched up with sepia washes, and the whole set was signed and numbered from nought to thirty-nine. I at once decided to show them to Gerhart Stolfzer, one of the most important contemporary picture-dealers, who immediately gave me a contract and implored me not to make the slightest change in my style - "You know, Sokolov, what the Americans are like these days ..." And so it happened that, in February 19--, I found myself reading an invitation card with the inscription: "Zumsteeg-Hauptmann Gallery, Gerhart Stolfzer requests the pleasure of your company at the private view of the work of the painter, Evguénie Sokolov." And although the latter was loathe to appear in public, he could not but attend.

Stolfzer introduced him to a number of pretty women, who irritated him profoundly by the stupidity of their pseudo-analytical remarks and so, executing a sharp volte-face, he farted full in their faces, so that his wind-bubbles, their stench partly mitigated by the perfumes emanating from the females, burst under the latter's noses and blended with the more acid bubbles from their champagne glasses.

Such a display of cheek and arrogance could not but appeal to them, but one female was overcome either by my smells or by the stuffiness of the room and collapsed, bringing down with her one of my engravings, the brittle glass of which shattered on hitting the floor and put out her left eye.

The incident was skillfully exploited to the best advantage by my dealer, whose brash personal assurance was no less remarkable than the size of the insurance claim he lodged with Lloyd's; he saw to it that we figured on the front pages of various mass-circulation papers, which gave a sensational account of the affair, as well as the most flattering photographic representation of Sokolov.

During the days that followed, the critics spoke about hyper-abstractionism, stylistic emphasis, formalistic mysticism, mathematical certainty, philosophical tension, exceptional eurhythmy and hypothetico-deductive lyricism, although a few also mentioned mystification, bluff and caca. Thirty-four of my works were sold in two weeks, mainly to Americans, Germans and Japanese; one went to the St. Thomas University Collection at Houston, another to the Bayerische Staatsgemäldesammlungen in Munich, and my stock rose like a bullet from a St. Etienne MAS 36, sighted at 1,200 meters and pointing straight towards the heavens.

This sudden notoriety caused me to be surrounded by willowy youths as fragile as April flowers, throbbing with suppressed and guilty urges, and by avid, passionate women who invited me to parties where my doggy alibi acted so often as a face-saver that, in gratitude, I stuffed the creature with various kinds of sweets, such as toffee, fruit-drops and fudge, until he began to look quite blown out and started to fart in real earnest. I would leave Mazeppa behind in the car only when we went to night-clubs, because there the electronic instruments vibrating powerfully at low frequencies, made it possible for me to break wind at will. Needless to say, I avoided first nights at the theater and the opera, to which dogs are never admitted.

It was about this time that I first began to have hemorrhages, a consequence no doubt of remaining too long in a sitting position.

That year, Stolfzer sold a hundred and one works by me, eighty-three drawings and engravings belonging to the gasogram series, and eighteen paintings, including one to the Detroit Institute of Arts, two to the Moderna Museet in Stockholm, one to the Marlborough Fine Arts Gallery in London, one to the Ateneum Art Museum in Helsinki, and finally a tryptich to the Stuttgart Staatsgalerie. At the same time, he managed to arrange exhibitions for me at the Galleria Galatea in Turin, the Crédit Communal de Belgique in Brussels and the University Art Museum at Berkeley.

I had numerous love affairs with members of both sexes since, partly through self-centredness and partly through fear of revealing my secret, I was unwilling to be tied down. I thus acquired a reputation as a brazen, cynical and fickle seducer but, becoming weary of operating on partners only moderately appreciative of my efforts or else afflicted with sodomitic anaphrodisia - "Not in there, Evguénie, you filthy bastard" - I eventually enjoyed more satisfaction with call girls and boys, who attended to my pleasure without my having to worry about theirs; sometimes I employed a group of these plump whores and beardless catamites because my rapidly blunted sensitivity needed the stimulus of hands with supernumerary fingers.

As regards my experience of passive homosexuality, it struck me as being of so little appeal that, in less than twenty seconds after the entry of the inquisitive organ, like a rocket launcher I shot it out again with one authoritative and definitive fart.

During this period of flatulent dandyism, my car was a six-and-a-half liter, black and steel-colored Bentley limousine, with Harrison body-work dating back to the nineteen-hundreds, and I left the driving to my valet who was separated from my effluvia by a glass partition, since I took care to keep him in ignorance of my disability and, as he was never allowed into my opisthodome at times of gaseous emission, he never suspected the use to which I put it.

He was, incidentally, a rather simple-minded young fellow, a sort of timid and apparently sexless Man-Friday, who occasionally broke his habitual silence to launch into incomprehensible jabberings about African magic and metamorphoses.

I sometimes got him to stop the car at the entrance-door of some rundown grand hotel, where I would take a suite for the night. First, I would wander through the deserted reception-rooms, listening to the tumultuous echo of my intestinal thunder among the Corinthian and Ionic capitals, or I would sit at the bar and get drunk on old-fashioned cocktails - Lady of the Lake, Baltimore Eggnog, Too Too, Winnipeg Squash, Horse's Neck, Tango Interval, White Capsule, Corpse Reviver, and my favorite Monna Vanna and Miss Duncan, pour without stirring equal parts of Cherry Brandy and green Curaçao into a small flute glass - and then, staggering under the combined effect of alcohol and sugar, I would lean against the inside wall of the lift and stare, glassy-eyed, at the floor-indicator.

My contract specified that I had to supply Stolfzer every month with fifteen drawings, engravings or paintings which, for the most part, he stashed away with speculative intent in his storerooms. It so happened that one morning, when I had got as far as my third sketch, and had my hand on the paper as I waited for the gaseous out burst, I experienced a slight feeling of anxiety which soon gave way to anguish, because not even the merest Khamsin or Aquilon seemed prepared to issue from within. All I achieved by the end of the day was a silent exhalation, as insubstantial as a sigh, which slipped from my fundament without causing the slightest perceptible oscillation in my hand. And the situation remained the same during the next few days; an occasional sirocco, but not a single resounding fart, with the result that the day before I was due to hand in my work, I had only three sketches ready for the dealer. I therefore asked him to allow me extra time, but unfortunately this was of no help. I then decided to rely entirely on my manual skill for the production of the gasograms. I worked at them frantically for a whole day and part of the night, but Stolfzer no sooner glanced at them then he frowned, gave a few negative shakes of the head and, before slamming the door behind him, declared peremptorily - using a traditional French expression - that they weren't worth a rabbit's fart, at which I first hiccoughed with desperate laughter and then fell into profound despair. It seemed, then, I had given up Crepitus Ventris, the jet-man who had ensured my livelihood for so long when I was still unknown, only to find

myself, now that I was famous, at the mercy of my intestinal whims. Two days later, I was awakened by a report so loud that it frightened my dog. I quickly slipped on a dressing gown and rushed to my easel. Dawn, a sublime dawn, was just breaking, and the silence was complete. Unfortunately, it lasted the whole day through and I did not leave my oscillometric seat until the sky was growing dark, but no sooner did I stand up than another grenade-like fart exploded under me. Such a total lack of synchronism and the ludicrousness of the situation set my nerves on edge. First I thought for a moment of blowing air into my anus with the aid of a bicycle pump, then I determined to procure medical text-books that would enlighten me about the nature of my disability and help me not to cure it, of course, but to cultivate it.

I managed to get hold of various studies: "Hysterical Types of Non-Gaseous Abdominal Bloating" by W.C. Alvarez, "The Volume and Composition of Colic Gases in Man" by A.F. Esbenkirk, "The Present Composition of Intestinal Gases, A Study of the Limits of Their Explosiveness When Mixed With Air" by Lambling and L. Truffert, "Diseases of the Intestine and the Peritoneum" by J. Rachet, A. Busson and C. Debray, "Clinical and Therapeutic Notes on Diseases of the Digestive System" by A. Mathieu and J.C. Roux, "Meteorism in Gastro-Intestinal Pathology" by J.C. Roux and F. Moutier, "Intestinal Gases, The Unsolved Aspects of a Bacteriological Problem" by A.R. Prévot, and "Concerning the Action of Post-Pituitary Extracts upon Gases in the Intestines" by A. Oppenheimer, and settled down to study them.

After noting in passing the exact composition of my gases - in every hundred cubic centimeters, sulphuretted hydrogen: random traces, carbon monoxide: nil, carbonic gas: 5.4%, hydrogen: 58.2%, hydrocarbides in the form of methane: 9.8%, and nitrogen: 26.4% - I went on to analyze the limits of explosiveness of mixtures of air and intestinal gases, also in terms of percentages of the gases - 7.5: explosion nil, 8.6: greatly delayed explosion, 9.9: slightly delayed explosion, 11.4, 13.2, 15.4, 24.6, 25.8, 27.5: immediate explosion, 28.6: explosion difficult, and 29.7: explosion nil, and then to discover the superb names of my most foul-smelling anaerobia: C. sprogenes, C. sordellii, C. bifermentans and C. putrificum. Going still further into the matter, I discovered that my intestines always contained a certain amount of gas, the function of which appeared twofold: to balance the atmospheric pressure and to stimulate and regulate the peristaltic movements; and also that the gases themselves were of three physiological kinds: gases exhaled from the blood towards intestinal light, swallowed air and gases produced by the digestive processes. Since the first appeared to play a minimal role, and the second to be only a very small proportion of the total, I decided to concentrate on the analysis of the gases produced by the digestive processes.

A small quantity of carbonic gas seemed to come from the neutralization of hydrochloric acid by the alkaline bases of the secretions present in the small intestine. In the latter part of this intestine, it would appear that normal microbes are active to ensure the digestion of cellulose and to complete the digestion of sugars and starches, with a consequent production of gases through acedic fermentation - hydrogen, carbon-

Evguénie Sokolov

ic gas and hydrocarbides - while other
microbic germs attack the amino acids
left over from the digestive process, or
the albuminoid secretions of the
mucous membrane, and these putrefaction processes give rise to ammonia,
hydrogen, methane, sulphuretted
hydrogen and carbonic gas.
Fermentation and putrefaction in the
caeco-colonic-rectal area being the
major source of intestinal gases, I realized the prime importance of my diet.

With feverish interest, I noted the
excess cellulose in pulses, green vegeta-
bles, coarse or strong-fibred fruit and
fresh or stale bread, as well as the large
quantity of starch in rice and pasta, and
I was struck by the usefulness of an
intake of partly decomposed proteins,
such as well-hung or even rotten meat,
offal, mushrooms and slightly "off" fish,

and after two weeks of concentrated dieting, I had the glass roof of the studio criss-crossed with strips of rubber-backed adhesive tape.

Soon there was a furious thundering of odorous farts, a remorseless blasting of anal gales and a wild pealing of chromatic flatulencies as the pressurized gases exploded into the open, to be drowned by Berg and Schönberg coming from record players turned up to maximum volume, while my hand sped over the paper as if I were suffering from paralysis agitans. But at the same time the atmosphere grew thick with strange aromas, rank essences, foul emanations, pestilential vapors, hallucinogenic miasmas, demoniacal perfumes and stenches of such putridity that I was on the point of giving up, when it occurred to me that somewhere in the cellars I had a gas mask of the ordinary civil defense type, which I had used in still life paintings during my Cubist period. Thereafter, I saw my graving-tools, pens and brushes only through the goggle-like apertures of this contraption, which separated me - who had now myself become a piece of living carrion - both from my smells and from the world at large.

Don your mask, Sokolov, and let your anaerobic fermentations blow the tubas of your fame and your irrepressible winds transform abscesses and ordinates into sublime anamorphoses!

In the space of four years, and quite unwittingly, I acquired followers, disciples and proselytes in Boston, NewYork, Philadelphia, Stuttgart, Amsterdam and Stockholm, and it was

Serge Gainsbourg

generally agreed that I was the out
standing representative of hyper-
abstractionism, the term invented by
the critic, Jacob Javits, after my first
exhibition. Certain art historians then
began to speculate about the problemat-
ic consequences of the movement and
even about the usefulness of its existence; they denied the seriousness of my
inspiration and asserted that Sokolov,
with his hysterical monotonousness,
was partly responsible for the tragic
stagnation, not to say retrograde development, of contemporary abstract art,
but their quibblings left me as unmoved
as Carrara marble, especially since they
were tedious to decipher and I punc-
tured the reading of them with vigor-
ous, spicy and avenging farts.

In any case, what did they matter? My work had now found its way

to the Tate Gallery in London, the Ulster Museum in Belfast, the Nationalgalerie in Berlin, the Yale University Art Gallery in Newhaven and the Museum of Modern Art in New York. Stolfzer sold it, as pricily as if it were platinum, to all the great tycoons, and some of my gasograms were now nonchalantly cradled in the bowels of splendid yachts, where their protective glass reflected both the silver glinting of cocktail shakers manipulated by barmen and the azure waters of floating swimming pools.

Fart, then, Sokolov onto that derisory world of luxury, and when the mirrors already fretted by your designs receive the super improved images of nymphets renewing their lipstick, may your ubiquitous presence serve as a multiple reflection of the vices of the earth. Oh Sokolov, your hyperacousia causes your hand to jolt. See, through the goggles of your mask, misted up with your high creative fever, how patterns and graphs come into being, as cathode ray tubes and modulation-monitors vacillate, writhe and fluoresce to the atonality of Berg and Schönberg, whose dodecacophonism joins in disharmony with your contrapuntal gases.

By now, blood spurted out with every bowel movement, scattering scarlet flowers over ivory lavatory bowls, but while I took an aesthetic interest in their patterns, I remained unmoved by the risk of eventual complications, although I was fully aware of them through having studied the medical text-books. Actually, being convinced of my exceptional destiny, I had difficulty in believing myself to be afflicted with any incurable complaint, and although the thought of consulting a proctologist occasionally crossed my mind, I very quickly dismissed it through fear of breaking wind in his face.

I must say a word here about my physical appearance, because it would be wrong for the reader, on reaching this point in my story, to imagine that I was careless in matters of personal hygiene, as he might be inclined to suppose in the case of someone exuding pestilential odors. I made ample use of bath oils, after-shave lotions and subtle, evanescent varieties of eau-de-Cologne, as well as of Extract of Cormoran Ylang-Ylang and Extract of Mysore Sandalwood that I had sent from Crabtree and Evelyn in Savile Row, but

I avoided heavy scents of animal origin which, on mixing with my gases, produced such dizziness and vomiting. My English tweed jackets were vomiting. My English tweed jackets were close-fitting and classical in style, because I wished to avoid the Bohemian look that certain artists indulge in. But my trousers were invariably American jeans, ample enough to facilitate ventilation. I wore no jewels or accessories, apart from a hexagonal watch that I kept concealed in my fob-pocket.

Some people might also think that so substantial a diet, rich in fats and protids, must have quickly affected my figure. Not at all. Being anxious to retain his original sliminess, Sokolov compelled himself to watch his weight and undertook forced marches, during which he became the dog and Mazeppa the master. We chatted analloquially, recalling with a few breezy farts bitches we had known and, to honor their memory, Mazeppa sprinkled the tires of parked cars with his teaming urine and then deposited a turd, punctuating its conical conclusion by spinning gleefully round and round.

Although I was weary of high society. I sometimes left my studio to seek nourishment in fashionable restaurants where, to kill time while my order was being dealt with, I made a mental note of that spent by different women in the lavatory; two minutes for urination and two minutes thirty seconds for the use of powder-puff, rouge and lipstick; beyond that limit, it seemed to me they must be engaged on more serious business; then, eyeing them as placidly as my dog did, I gauged the extent of their embarrassment, which was in inverse ratio to the time that had elapsed. In these restaurants, my favorite food was poultry, ortolans, larks, thrushes, partridges, doves, ptarmigan, grouse, capercaillies, moorhens, pheasants and snipe, resting on a bed of braised cabbage or on a purée of yellow, red, kidney or butter beans. As regards cheese, I ignored the double cream varieties, Sarah, Chester, Cheddar, Stilton and Gouda, judging their fragrance too subtle, in order to concentrate on the ammoniacal effluvia of cancoillotte, géromé, Munster, boulette d' Avesnes, livarot and maroilles, as well as Corsican cheese from the Nialo area and vieux Lille, also known as "macerated stinker", and I must say that an immediate contact was established between these varieties of carnal and lactic decay, my Havana cigars, my intestinal gases and my immediate neighbors, and that it was rendered all the more excruciating by my phlegmatic silence and imperturbable facial expression.

One evening, when I was trucking into a grouse in an advanced state of decomposition and had just ordered a few swizzle-sticks-to release gases from the fundament is one thing, to bring them up in belches due to champagne is another, and too frequent in my view - I heard to the right a series of reports which could certainly not originate from my dog, which was lying next to my left foot. They occurred in sequence as if they were coming from beneath the tail of a horse moving at a gentle trot, and the gamey odor produced was reminiscent of that which precedes the ejection of equine droppings. The detonating diner, munching his solitary way through a lobster, was an extremely elegant, bony-faced man of about fifty, with whom I immediately started hostilities and, after an initial exchange of brisk artillery fire, followed on his part by salvoes from a heavy machine-gun and on mine by the bursting of a few, well aimed hand grenades, firing became more intermittent, the two strategists decided on an armistice, and negotiations began at the oral level. I learned that my opposite number was called Arnold Drupp, that he was a surgeon by profession and, in addition, collected pictures and engravings by modern masters and had in his possession, amongst other things, two Klees, three Picabias and nine Sokolovs. For my part, thinking it unwise to reveal my identity, because I might perhaps let myself in for another lecture, from him I mean, on the hyper-abstractionist movement, I introduced Mazeppa and then sat down again, with a consequent depression and explosion of a cushion of fetid air. By the time we got to the coffee, we were discussing Dada. It was soon the turn of the Surrealists, who accompanied the liqueurs, while the hyper-abstractionists came with the cigars, which we had however some difficulty in lighting in the gale-like force of our reciprocal windiness. "I think", Krupp announced suddenly, "that two of my Sokolovs are fakes. Just ordinary electrocardiograms," he explained, directing towards me a stare oxidized by alcohol. I responded with a smile of gentian blue, "Doctor, you have in your possession gasograms number one hundred and one and one hundred and two, the only ones ever done by Sokolov on the rolls of graph-paper used by cardiologists." "A hundred and one, and a hundred and two", Arnold Krupp exclaimed, "You're right, exactly right! My dear sir, I suppose you must be a ..." "Oh, as for me", I replied as I took my leave, "I disguise myself as a man so as to be nothing (Picabia, Jesus Christ, Rastaquouère)." Nevertheless, I accepted the visiting-card he pressed upon me in so imperatively cordial a manner, while at the same time wondering how it was that the flaunted flatulence of this repulsive art-lover did not affect the movement of his scalpel during delicate operations.

In the autumn of 19--, at Stolfzer's insistence, I agreed, though unwillingly, to go to Zurich to do a series of frescoes for a film producer

named Loewy, who had just built himself a splendid residence of concrete,
steel and reinforced glass on the slopes
overlooking the lake. My task was to
run my gasograms along the walls of an
immense hall, which had in its center a
baptistery surrounded by columns with
composite capitals, and the mosaic
pavement of which could be raised to
form a dancing floor. This octagonal
swimming pool was empty for the time
being, and the hall unoccupied, so that
the echo, which was as lively as any to
be found in a gramophone recording
studio, rebounded in waves under the
immense glass vault. Foreseeing the
dangers of the undertaking, I demand-
ed that a team of workmen should go
up onto the roof and fix bands of adhesive tape over it in X and Z shapes, on
the pretext that the harsh light, which

was in danger of blunting my judgment, would thereby be softened to some degree. My host complied, taking my request to be no more than the whim of an eccentric genius. Finally, after receiving an assurance that no one would disturb me on any account, apart from my valet who would be responsible for my diet, Mazeppa's outings and the making of the camp-bed I had had set up in the swimming pool, I climbed up my aluminum scaffolding, settled myself on my oscillometric seat, and began to spread the first wash.

Soon, in a thunder of farts echoed a hundred fold by the glass roof and the marble paving, my black lines began to zigzag over the inner surface of this new Sistine Chapel, cracking the walls as if through the effect of earth-tremors. Then, one day, just after a

tremendous blast had pushed me thirty
centimeters forward and I had drawn
back a little in order to appraise the sub-
tlety of the pattern produced, I had a
sudden and disturbing intuition of
another presence. I turned round, and
into the visual field of my goggles
swam a little girl, sitting on my bed in
the baptistery and gazing at me with
large, unmoving eyes. Sokolov experienced a fit of giddiness which almost
toppled him off his scaffolding. I
released a sorry fart, wrenched off my
gas mask, walked unsteadily to the
edge of the empty swimming pool and,
after some initial hemming and hawing,
asked her who she was and what she
was doing there, but her features, which
were particularly delicate and beautiful
under the platinum waves of her hair,
remained as motionless as if they had

been molded in polyester. In a voice broken by shame, I repeated my questions, uttering each syllable distinctly in the confused hope of finding some undeveloped, rudimentary creature at my feet, and it was then that the corners of her mouth curled up slowly into a smile. This diabolical child had obviously discovered my appalling secret. In my panic, it occurred to me to open the water-valves of the swimming pool, but she suddenly took a notebook from her pocket, wrote something on a page which she held up for me to see, and beckoned me to come down. After joining her, I was able to read the following words, painstakingly inscribed in green ink: "My name is Abigail. I am eleven years old". After a moment's hesitation, I borrowed her notebook and pen: "The nasty smells you may notice, Abigail,

are only due to the chemical composition of my paints." It is quite likely that
the exact meaning of this message
escaped her, at the same time as a force-
four wind escaped from me, but the
charming little girl smiled at me so gra-
ciously that my mood changed abruptly
from sepia to Prussian blue and, little
by little and day by day, as she made
use of sheets from her notebook and I of
a para-language composed of gestures,
mimicry and grimaces, there grew out
of our silences, which were disturbed
only by the scraping of her pen and the
explosion of my gases, a sublime, secret
and tender feeling, the painful stigmata
of which I still bear in my heart and in
my lower parts. Abigail acquired the
habit of coming every day to sit on my
bed in the swimming pool to nibble
rusks or marie-biscuits, and at night I

could feel against my skin the crumbs that had escaped her childish teeth and which stimulated my criminal desires, inflaming my insomnia with congestive erections. I showed her my way of drawing sewing needles in a single movement, and the smaller I made the eye, the more pronounced her soundless laughter, and the more enthusiastically she clapped her applause as she threw herself backwards on my bed.

One night, she came to slip her tender gosling-flesh against mine in the Arctic cold of the great hall, and thus it was that, on a camp-bed in an empty swimming-pool lit by a blur of starlight, I uttered the only words of love I have ever used in my life into the ear of a little deaf-mute. In my frenzy, I combined them with appalling obscenities which came from my clenched jaws as if I

were a ventriloquist, while little
Abigail, in breathless excitement and
instinctive attempts at orgasm, writhed
and howled in silence beneath me.
Through fear of the apparently immi-
nent expulsion of a rush of wind, which
pierced my bowels at the very moment
when I was about to expire with
delight, and the stench of which I had
reason to fear, I interrupted the act of
congress and repressed my orgasm with
bitter tears. The few grams and milli-
liters of sperm involved went backup
into my brain, doing it serious damage,
the effects of which I still experience in
the form of blinding flashbacks. For a
long time, I tried unavailingly to burst
the abcess inflaming my brain by means
of brisk masturbation, but the luke-
warm curdled milk which emerged was
never the same as the scalding liquid of

that exemplary evening. The next day, Abigail went off to boarding school. I hastily completed the rest of my corrosive patterning in forty-eight hours, and left Zurich.

After this encounter, I remained incapable of painting for six months. It was during this period of manual inactivity that I hit on the sad notion of recording my flatulency, which now had the silent sound of tear gas, with Hi-Fi equipment, and the first playbacks plunged me, alternately, into two very different states. In the first, I would invent an acoustic illustration to a cartoon based on Crepitus Ventris, the Jet-Man, and I would imagine my hero flying up through the cumulus clouds, rising to the cirro-stratus and, with one anal burst, leaving lyre-jets far behind; then, he would either switch off his engine and dive back to earth, or, increasing the fuel-feed, leave long, firey, anal traces in the sky; and such was my exultation that my old laughter would return and swamp my tearful gaze with hallucinatory, submarine visions, and sometimes even the viscous humor would swell out of my nostrils in opalescent globes, from which slugs emerged as if from chrysalises. In the second, I would be transported by the symphonic concert, and would sink into a heavy, melomaniacal and tetanic lethargy. Once he had recovered from these extreme, trance-like states, Sokolov set about superimposing on his existing tapes additional recordings made with tuba, bass trombone, bugle and ophicleide, the sound quality and melodic phrasing of which he varied at will through controlled relief of the gaseous pressures in the larger and smaller intestines, thus producing a shattering symphony that sounded as if it were being conducted by some water-diviner brandishing his rod, or had been put together like the firing-instructions to the howitzers and muskets of West Point Military Academy used for the recording of the battle of Vittoria. The performance set Mazeppa howling to the death and gave Sokolov the idea of making multiple gasograms, similarly elaborated by means of successive operations.

Thus began first the sketches, then the studies, for the electrocuted zebra, now to be seen in the Solomon R. Guggenheim Museum in New York. These studies were the subject of a new exhibition organized by Stolfzer.

That evening, for the first time, I

allowed myself to be interviewed by a journalist. The din in the gallery was such that I thought it would drown the noise of my flatulence, which had become increasingly uncontrollable. But the questions asked by the N.B.C. reporter were of the insidious kind, such as: "Sokolov, what is your political position about art?" Irritated by the aggressive interrogation and bothered by the glaring camera lights, I parried at first with laconic sentences delivered in peremptory tones; no, I was not only particularly interested in knowing whether I had any influence on contemporary painting; yes, of course, I was acquainted with the suicidal works of Schasberg, Krantz, Gulenmaster, Högenolf, Wogel and other jokers; no, I was not greatly impressed by what they were doing, and then, when he tried to corner me by means of more perfidious questions, I suddenly realized that the onlookers had fallen silent, having become intrigued by the pugnacious tone of my replies. Feeling myself doomed in the now total quiet, I assumed an icy look and said: "Mr. Intellectual, about my painting, let me just say this" and, snatching the microphone from him, I put it smartly to my fundament and produced a report of such density that I could feel the feces dribbling down my legs. The spectators recoiled, suffocated by the smell, while the sound-engineer, standing next to the camera and no doubt with the needle of his sound-meter stuck at more than three decibels, staggered under the impact of the gas injected directly into his brain through the headphones.

American T.V. broadcast the

interview in full, that is, fart included, and sold the film throughout the world, so that it was shown far and wide, its multiple performances creating a chain-reaction in which my wind acquired the force of a nuclear explosion which shook the whole globe.

The newspapers seized on the scandal, with such inane headlines as "Hyper-abstraction Nothing But Wind"; my canvases sold like hot cakes, at the rate of 16,000 dollars *le point*, or unit of surface measurement, and Stolfzer rubbed his hands together more vigorously than ever. As for myself, noticing that the bleedings were getting worse, I became jumpy, tetchy, somber, incapable of sleep and vile to my dog, which I constantly kicked about, until one day, when I was thoroughly ashamed of myself, I happened to light on the visiting-card of the surgeon, Arnold Krupp, who recommended me, under a false name of course, to a proctologist friend of his; I immediately went to consult this specialist and, after a painful digital examination, he diagnosed large internal hemorrhoids.

A week later, the pain became so unbearable that I agreed to go to the hospital for intrarectal electrocoagulation treatment. In fact, I had the treatment twice and now, as I write these words, I am waiting in the hospital bed to have it a third time.

On the first occasion, which was preceded by a rapid examination of the lesions, the treatment triggered off an explosion which blew the anal speculum and the electrical instrument out of the doctor's hands. On the second, after the initial part of the operation had been completed normally, the last application of the instrument caused a flame to shoot out of the anal speculum, setting fire to a cotton-wool swab held by a nurse standing two paces back and spraying the surgeon's face and beard with particles of fecal matter. I became aware of the incident only through the doctor's hasty retreat. I fell into a faint; my pulse became erratic and I had to be given restorative and cardiotonic injections.

      This was too humiliating to be borne, and so I decided to put an end to my deplorable and aromatic existence. As regards the method, I first thought of veronal, but then it seemed only logical to commit suicide through inhaling intestinal gas. I therefore procured a yard of rubber tubing, made an incision in the fabric of my gas mask, connected up one end of the tube and secured it with adhesive tape. Then, after smearing the other end with Vaseline, I inserted it into my rectum. "Your life is over, Sokolov", I said to myself as I breathed in my intestinal gas, "You have lived out your unspeakable destiny. But what fear can death hold for you, who during your lifetime were nothing but fermentation and putrefaction, recorded, codified and charted for all time by your prophetic hand!"

My valet, who was responsible for my reprieve, found me lying unconscious on the floor of the studio, just when I was about to choke to death on the vomit that had filled my gas mask right up to the eyepieces. However, he remained ignorant of the full scope of my ingenuousness since, fortunately, and no doubt because of some convulsive movement during my unconscious discomfort, I had lost the length of tubing fitted to my rectum.

Now began the series of orchidaceous patterns, the product of a manic-depressive breakdown and of a very simple technique, similar to that which women use to reduce the shininess of their lipstick. After each stool, I applied sheets of tissue-paper to the crack between my buttocks. I had to use five or six sheets before all traces of excrement disappeared, after which I obtained the definitive print of the rayed folds of my bleeding anus, a star-like print which varied according to the openness of the inner and outer sphincters, the pressure of my fingers, the emission or non-emission of wind during the operation and the intensity of the bleeding.

Serge Gainsbourg

After the blood had coagulated and the sheets had been mounted, each on a crimson velvet background, under glass and in a gilded frame, I instructed my engraver to inscribe the titles of my works in lower-case italic script - the most austere form of lettering, in my view - on brass plaques to be attached to the bases of the frames: "Self-Portrait One", "Self-Portrait Two", and so on; these titles infuriated the critics even more than the works themselves.

"Evguénie", Stolfzer said to me on the day after the private view, as he deposited photocopies of the hostile press reactions on my table - I glanced at them: Sokolov the Magnificent, Hottento, Adonis, Scarface, Anthropometric Police File, Fall-Out From Dada, Shit-Stars- "Evguénie, I've got you an official commission, an embassy ceiling in Moscow. I know how extremely allergic you are to traveling, but you must understand that we can't turn down such an important offer. Think of the Tretiakov Gallery". Having made this absurd remark, he left.

Was I supposed to express myself in my capacity as gasographer, in which case I could hardly imagine myself perched on my oscillometric seat, with my right arm stretched straight upwards and my face all spattered with sepia at the first explosion. On the other hand, if I were to keep to my latest manner, what Boschian acrobatics would be required to enable me to apply my fundament on the surface of a Moscow ceiling?

The solution occurred to me at daybreak, after one of the sleepless nights caused by my mounting fear of a further spell in the hospital. I covered two hundred and fifty sheets of glazed paper with a mixture of alum, aluminum oxide and gum tragacanth, carefully numbered them on the back, then produced the same number of orchidaceous patterns on tissue paper and transferred them, one by one and before they had time to dry, onto the already prepared sheets. Once the bloody transposition had been achieved, all Sokolov had to do was to send off the jigsaw puzzle to Moscow, in the care of a student of the Ecole des Beaux Arts who had instructions to moisten the prints before applying them to the ceiling in a stated order of numbering, and then to take each one down after a few seconds' contact.

Some time later, I received a telephone call from an attaché at the Moscow Embassy: "By the way, Mr. Sokolov, what is the title of your painting?" After a moment's reflection, I replied: "Decalcomania", between two farts, and hung up. As if through some appalling phenomenon of mimeticism, no sooner had I uttered the word than Mazeppa, after emptying the wind from his guts in a prolonged and sinister cannonade, rolled over on his side and gave up his ghost to me.

"Abigail", I immediately cried, as my eyes filled with scalding tears, "would that I could insert between my buttocks, not a shepherd's pipe as shown in that remarkable detail of the picture of the Garden of Delights in the Prado, but an ultrasonic whistle which, at the first breath, would pierce your deafness, so that you would perhaps come back to me, like a bitch in hea..."

Sokolov's notebooks were discovered by the house doctor under his hospital bed two days after the fatal accident, which occurred during intrarectal electrocoagulation when the explosion of the intestinal gases of the patient resulted in a major rupture of the sigmoid.

Certain details, however, need to be made clear. First of all, the fact that the explosion did not happen in the first stage of the electrocoagulation process, but only in the third, after an interval which had allowed air to penetrate into the rectal cavity. The intra-abdominal explosion was not accompanied, as one might suppose, by an immediate pain, comparable to the sudden stab characteristic of a perforation. The pelvic pain came on a little later, and gradually increased. This pain was never in syncopation; it continued for a few hours in successive waves, like the pangs of uterine colic, separated by phases of sedation during which the patient twice fell into a doze. The sensation seemed so bearable to him that it took all the doctors' authority to convince him that he should go home in an ambulance. His state was such that it was possible to carry out a check with the anal speculum, and this revealed neither any mucous lesion due to burning nor any trace of blood. At no time immediately following the accident was the stomach distended with wind. On the contrary, it was flat, and remained supple for more than three and a half hours. No symptom of shock was noticeable; the patient had a slightly congested look, but otherwise his facial expression was normal; his pulse was steady, although rather quick, and his breathing calm.

At this point, Sokolov, according to his valet, gave instructions for the writing of a note which was to be handed to Stolfzer on the day of his funeral, which he felt to be fast approaching. His condition deteriorated rapidly and soon all the symptoms indicated peritonitis resulting from perforation. The patient was operated on at three o'clock in the morning, and stitches were put into the sigmoid to repair the sixteen centimeter, ragged-edged tear. A few clots of blood were discovered in the peritoneum and, what was more serious, numerous traces of fecal matter in the whole of the abdominal cavity and even under the liver, a circumstance which did not leave much room for hope. And, in fact, Sokolov passed away thirteen hours after the operation, and twenty hours after the accident, with all the signs of hyper toxic peritonitis, the seriousness of his state being emphasized by a vomito negro, which occurred at the beginning of the afternoon, although there had been an apparent abatement of the symptoms during the morning. The official autopsy confirmed the existence of the lesions noted at the time of the operation, as well as the quite normal extent and appearance of the therapeutic coagulation of the tumoral hemorrhoids.

Two days later, hydrogen plus oxygen in contact with a naked flame amounted to an explosive gas. Just as one of the gravediggers was about to throw down the first shovelful of earth, and Gerhart Stolfzer, complying with the wishes expressed in the artist's note,

put a light to a cigar, there was a muf-
fled report which lifted the lid of the
coffin. Evguénie Sokolov had just
breathed his final anal sigh, and rendered a last, gaseous, posthumous, poi-
sonous salute to the memory of
mankind.

An Afterword...

With Serge Gainsbourg's then current lover Babou looking on, I tried hard not to stare at the nude Polaroid's of his ex-wife Jane Birkin affixed to the walls of his Casino de Paris dressing room after his September 1985 concert. I asked Gainsbourg if he had any intention of trying to duplicate his phenomenal French success by performing in America. He quickly replied, "Why bother, they wouldn't understand."

Regarding France, we Americans understand the Eiffel Tower, the baguette, and the beret. Yet a character as complex and French as Gainsbourg, is much harder to 'get.' In America, we don't have 60 year old pop-singer/composers who are still at the height of their creativity and still considered edgy and

Russell Mael

cool. And, who are adored by both the
intelligentsia and the masses. This ain't
no Barry Manilow. It seemed like the
more Gainsbourg provoked, the more
debauched he acted, the more irreverent
he was, the more he was loved. His
sudden death at the age of 62 saddened
an entire nation, and myself.

He turned his country's national
anthem, La Marseillaise, into a contro-
versial reggae hit which took France by
storm. The sensual moaning of real-life
lover Jane Birkin helped propel his
Chopin prelude inspired
"JeT'Aime...Moi Non Plus" to interna-
tional success despite being banned by
even that old arbiter of good taste, the
BBC. He wrote and produced songs for
(and had romantic liaisons with) a vir-
tual Who's Who of French actresses
from Bardot to Deneuve to Adjani. He

appeared in a video for a song he authored for his daughter Charlotte called "Lemon Incest." The panty-clad teenage girl sang the song from her bed as her shirtless father looked on, also lying in that same bed. The innuendo was hardly concealed. The record sold like Petits-pains. And on a French chat show the equivalent of our 'Tonight Show', the guest of honor Gainsbourg appeared sporting his trademark three day growth of facial hair. During the live interview he uttered in English about the show's other guest Whitney Houston, "I want to fuck her." The startled host of the show tried to diffuse the comment by translating it to his viewers as "Serge says he would like to offer you some flowers." To which Serge replied in French, "No I said I would like to fuck her."

And despite all of Gainsbourg's showbiz and personal quirks the French Minister of Culture Jack Lang awarded him the Croix d'Officier de L'Ordre des Arts et Des Lettres, a prestigious cultural prize. You would've had to be there to understand.

About his 1980 "conte parabolique" Evguénie Sokolov, Gainsbourg told emanate from the reader's mouth was nervous laughter, as this was a tragic tale to the extreme. He said the story was autobiographical, yet with "distortions reminiscent of Francis Bacon's paintings. Evguénie is a guy who knowingly destroyed himself because he wanted fame, and that fame destroyed him."

As the Casino de Paris house lights dimmed and the concert began, a silhouette of Gainsbourg puffing on a cigarette appeared atop an extremely high staircase. A Las Vegas entrance, if ever there was one. Then to the horror and bewilderment of us all, the figure stumbled on the steps and tumbled all the way to the floor, lying there motionless as a shocked silence filled the hall. From the wings, a spotlight caught the entrance of the 'real' Gainsbourg while his stunt double picked himself up off the floor and scurried offstage. The concert began thus, and the audience's response was that same nervous laughter that Gainsbourg spoke of for "Evguénie Sokolov."

Russell Mael
Sparks
Los Angeles, April 1998